How To
Date A
Vampire

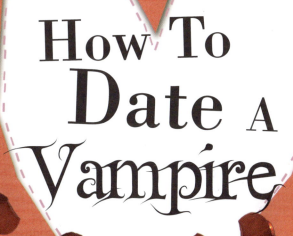

How To Date A Vampire

Sophie Collins

spruce

An Hachette UK Company

First published in Great Britain in 2009 by Spruce,
a division of Octopus Publishing Group Ltd
2–4 Heron Quays, London E14 4JP
www.octopusbooks.co.uk
www.octopusbooksusa.com

Distributed in the U.S. and Canada for Octopus Books USA
c/- Hachette Book Group USA
237 Park Avenue
New York NY 10017

ISBN-13: 978-1-84601-352-2
ISBN-10: 1-84601-352-6

A CIP catalog record of this book is available from
the Library of Congress.

Printed and bound in China

10 9 8 7 6 5 4 3 2 1

Contents

Introduction

We'll get to the "how" in a second, but let's deal with a more important question first. Why do you want to date a vampire?

Could it be to do with the hugely improved PR the undead have had recently? Have you finally woken up to their darkside charm, their supernatural intelligence, and their unearthly good looks? Are you the kind of girl who hankers after a bad-boy date? Buffy and Bella got it right—now you too can date the undead and enjoy the experience!

We'll take you through every stage of the relationship: where to find your fangsome fella, how to catch his eye (in the right way, naturally) and ways to swap and share your interests.

We don't shrink from the knottier questions, either. What are the best ways to get him to hang with your gang? What should you do when meeting his? Plus the perfect presents to give and get, great dates (and definite no-nos), and how to deal with vamp living as you guys get closer.

We've even given you a crash course in crypt culture with a look at vamp history's biggest names and the top ten vampire movies of all time. And, while we don't want to rain on your vampire parade, you'll find plenty of safety advice along the way. After all, when you're looking for love, you don't want to end up as lunch.

BEFORE YOU START OUT

Woah girl! You probably want to get out there right now and bag yourself a vamp, but here's some stuff to remember. Stay safe, and have fun!

★ Take a warm jacket (getting close to a chilly guy is nice on a hot summer's night, but less refreshing when there's a cold wind blowing).

★ Apply a liberal spritz (or seven) of your fave perfume. You don't want to smell too, well, human, amongst vamps you don't know and trust.

★ Start your search with an upbeat attitude. Vampires have suffered from a poor press for centuries; now that they're finally getting dates on a Friday night, you can help by looking at the plus points of this very special sort of cross-species squeeze.

Love at First Bite

Vampires are all different, just like human boys, so dive in to discover which vamp's for you! We'll tell you where to find his favorite haunts, how to wow his crowd, and all the savviest responses to his killer chat-up lines.

Learn to read his body language (there's more at stake, in every sense, than with a regular boy) and, best of all, see how to blag his perfect style. Now go get your vampire!

Stake Outs: Finding Your Vampire

You'll have read about vampires hunting people, but how do you turn the tables and pursue your own pale 'n' interesting boy? Well, first things first...you've got to know where to look. Try these likely hangouts:

Indie movie club

Lots of vampires like cult horror movies—and vampire flicks in particular. They enjoy counting up the mistakes that we make about them on celluloid.

Join the club, go to the next vampire/zombie double bill and sit next to the gorgeous guy with the slight smile playing around his bloodless lips.

Caving/Potholing

If you don't mind getting into tight spots, these are sports that vampires are suckers for. They take you to cold, dark, bat-filled places; they call for endurance and agility; and the ability to see in the dark is a definite advantage. Rope yourself to the boy who looks as though he's already spent a few hours underground.

Latin dancing

Not for the faint hearted, but neither's dating the undead! Tango and salsa have a powerful pull for vampires: with their fabulous rhythm, the hot Latin dances give them the chance to get up-close and personal with gorgeous warm-blooded girls.

If you've always wanted to work on your rumba, visit your local Latin class. Take a look at the instructors: this has been known as a career choice for vampire couples.

Costume store

With their killer looks and inbuilt elegance, most vampires love to dress up, but their modern lifestyles mean that most days they're wearing jeans and tees like the other boys. Hang out at your local costume store and see if you can spot a guy who's a natural for evening dress. Don't kid around with the plastic fangs, though – he won't think it's funny.

AVOID!

Even though they might seem obvious vampire hot-(or cold-)spots, don't make the mistake of hanging around graveyards at night.

Not only are they damp and scary, but most modern-thinking vampire boys have moved on. You're more likely to run into a ghoul or ghost, and you want a squeeze with a bit more substance.

Seven Deadly Chat-Up Sins

Butterflies in your belly? Sweaty palms? Mouth gone dry? You must be face to face with a vamp-boy! Your heart might be pounding and your pulse racing, but avoid these seven deadly chat-up sins and you'll soon have killer convo skills.

Pride

Everyone's got some cringey chat-up tales to tell, but if you dwell on them you'll never turn them into success stories, and practice makes perfect. So swallow your pride and take a risk. Everybody loves to know they're liked. He's only human, after all (sort of…)!

Lust

Hands on hips and a poser's pout isn't super-sexy—it's screaming, "Beware, I've got attitude!" Newsflash: vamps get enough soulless stares at home!

Make yourself as fun and approachable as possible. Keep your arms unfolded and, most importantly, smile! Make sure it's genuine, though, or he'll think you're making fun of his fangs!

Anger

Don't beat yourself up! You might not be that confident, but vamps are surrounded by dark thoughts 24-7. To be a breath of fresh air, try a sunny disposition. Picture yourself at your most vamp-slaying hilarious and he'll be putty in your pretty hands.

Greed

There's nothing wrong with watching and learning from other girls, but be picky about your approach! Mix and match what you've seen work with what suits your personality. It doesn't take a psychic to see when someone's not being themselves.

Gluttony

You might have a million things you want to say to him, but don't get a case of the verbal runs! Remember, everything in moderation.

Work out what you want from your tête-à-tête. We're not talking cue cards, but starting with an idea of where you want your chat to go helps to make it happen!

Envy

Jealous of his cool charisma and laid-back look? Tempted to be more like him? Stop! Vamps aren't used to seeing their reflections, so a mirror-image of them isn't going to appeal. Plus, their psychic powers mean nothing's sexier to them than a girl who knows her own mind.

Don't be afraid of standing up for your views, even if they're different from his. Opposites attract!

Sloth

Getting a vampire to talk about himself is far from easy, but keep at it! The best way to win a boy over is to show a genuine interest in him and what he's about. And it works for you, too. You've spent enough time daydreaming about him, after all! Share his passions, and you'll soon be one of them!

Vampire Icebreakers

Whether you're at the cinema, out dancing, or simply hanging out after school, you've spotted someone. Pale as the grave with good looks to die for? He *must* be a vamp. Then your eyes meet and he comes over. First lines matter. What's he going to choose for an icebreaker?

Here are some winning lines, and a few shockers that should send you sprinting for the door.

Green light: Go! Go! Go!

Regular guys could learn a lot from a vampire's moves with a girl he likes the look of. This boy has more years of experience than most and knows simplicity works. A smile and a "Hey" are worth any number of cheesy chat-up techniques.

On the other hand, lines that might sound corny from a regular date— "You're the cutest girl I've seen in a century!"—just might be a straight-up truth from a vampire. Don't dismiss them straight off; a girl can always stick around to hear *one* more…

Red light: No! No! No!

Sure, girls love the limelight now and then, but take care with a vamp. You want his attention, but you don't want things to get out of control, even if he makes your heart race from across the room.

When you hear lines like "You smell good enough to eat" or "Your pulse is beating so fast I can actually hear it," they aren't good signals. Add a dark and unblinking gaze and…uh-oh. This isn't just a compliment on your choice of perfume: this is a vampire checking out his next meal.

BEWARE OF BORES!

Human or vampire, there are lines no girl should fall for:

★ "Are you tired? 'Cause you've been running through my head all day!"

★ "When God made you he was showing off!"

These guys aren't dangerous in the blood-drinking sense, but the boredom might finish you off.

Quiz: What Sort of Vampire is He?

Vampires on TV might seem all bats, capes, and coffins, but what about the guy you only just met, who happens to have dead-white skin and a taste for super-rare steak? To work your way into his heart, you'd better start with his head. Choose the answers below that fit him best, then turn the page to crack his character.

1 How would you sum up his style?
a. Scruffy but sexy; well-practised grunge. ☆
b. Gorgeously gothic, with carefully chosen accessories. ☆
c. Total punk rebel; easy to spot in a crowd. ☆
d. The boy next door—to die for! ☆

2 At school, you catch sight of him outside the principal's office…*again*. What's his crime?
a. He's probably been cutting class again. ☆
b. Refusing a locker check. (What's he hiding in there?) ☆
c. Cheating on a test. His answers were faultless. ☆
d. You heard he was just looking out for his mate. ☆

3 Which type of movie does he prefer?
a. Cult classics and all-time greats. ☆
b. Black and white, arthouse, covered in subtitles. ☆
c. Pure horror—anything with screaming blond girls. ☆
d. Comedy or comic-book: he'll try anything once. ☆

4 At a party, where are you most likely to find him?
a. He *is* the party! DJ-ing, with the band or in the band, he's always the center of attention. ☆
b. In a corner, watching the night unfold. ☆
c. Slow dancing with another girl… How many is that now? ☆
d. Chatting with a couple of close friends. ☆

5 When you catch him looking at you, where's his gaze fixed?
a. He's openly admiring your butt. ☆
b. Hard to say—you can't seem to follow his eyes. ☆
c. Your neck. He can't tear his eyes away from your pulse. ☆
d. Your eyes. You could drown in his gaze. ☆

6 What drives you wild about him?
a. Everyone just wants to be near him. Including you! ☆
b. You can't work him out, but it's fun trying. ☆
c. He's just the kind of guy that your parents would *hate*. ☆
d. You just don't understand—how can you feel such a strong connection with someone so distant? ☆

Answers: What Sort of Vampire is He?

Mostly As

He's a fly-by-night fella! Being part of this toothsome twosome is a rollercoaster ride. Fun, funky, and incredibly sexy, he's always surrounded by a posse of pals...and girls. He's a nonstop partygoer with an awesome amount of energy, but if you can get close, his heart's definitely in the right place.

Mostly Bs

He's a Mr. Mystery: a man of few words, but many secrets. Quiet, shy, and often serious, he's learned a lot in his long past and it's made him reflective (although not in front of mirrors). But that doesn't mean he's miserable. Lending a listening ear could help soothe his tortured soul, and although it takes a lot of work, once you've melted his heart, it will be all yours.

Mostly Cs

He's tall, dark...and dangerous. Hang on to your crucifix and grab some garlic. You might think this vamp boy's sweet underneath, but he's only after one thing...the bite. His seduction routine might be delicious, but he'll love you and leave you once he's had his fill, so steer clear of this one. Find yourself a veggie vamp instead.

Mostly Ds

Congratulations—you've struck gold and located a lifetime lover. Cute, charismatic, and deadly sexy, the most frustrating thing about this vampire is that he doesn't realize he's driving you crazy. For all his years of immortality he's still too shy to make the first move with a girl he thinks the world of, but once he's gained your trust he'll be totally loyal and supportive. Just be sure you're ready for the responsibility of being his everything.

Dating your Vampire

Not *that* sort of dating! This is about finding out how long your renegade has been around, aged eternally 17. He isn't a tree, so you can't count his rings, and looking at his teeth is a bit too perilous. "How old are you?" is a rude question for vamps (almost the only thing they have in common with your grandma), so he won't be bragging about it on his blog.

Here are some neat (and only slightly underhand) ways to hunt for clues.

Leading questions

If you can't try a direct question, something subtler may unlock his secret. This is easy as pie if you share history or literature classes with your new crush.

He'll want to impress you, so a question or observation—something like, "How do you think they really built the pyramids?" or "I like Jane Austen, but I can't believe that girls didn't just speak their minds back then!"—may tempt him to reveal his inside knowledge.

Once it's clear that he's talking from memory, not just guesswork, you can gently probe for more details. He'll seem even more romantic when you learn that he spent time with the pharaohs 5000 years ago, or danced at full-dress balls in Charleston before the Civil War.

Surprising skills

Keep a sharp eye out for special expertise your vamp possesses (that's above and beyond the laser sight, super smell, sonic hearing, and flying, of course). Vamps are chronic hoarders who love to impress, just like ordinary guys, but have had more than a lifetime to learn to show off.

Try asking where (and when) he got his expertise. Dancing, archery, fencing, even cooking skills above and beyond the norm, can all offer leads on your vamp's mysterious past.

Vintage vamp

Further clues to his start date may be found in your guy's dress sense. Even though the modern undead wear the same clothes as us, they always have a private retro penchant for the styles they grew up with.

You may find that your fella tends toward vintage stores and the 19th century, or shows most interest when a costume party themed to the roaring 20s comes along. Ask him when he wishes he'd grown up—and you may find out when he actually did!

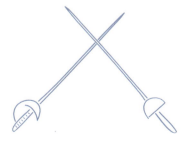

Reading your Vamp's Body Language

You know he can read your mind, literally, but if you learn to spot the giveaways in your vamp's demeanor, you'll find your female intuition more than a match for his supersenses. Find out what's hot and what's not in your vamp's body language. Girl power in its strongest form!

What's hot?

His eyes

With your regular guy, his eyes are the giveaway. If he can look you straight in the eye, all's well and he's telling the truth. With a vampire, things are different. This guy doesn't even need to blink, so holding

When you say grab a bite...?

I swear I didnt mean you...

your gaze is simply second nature. While his eyes stay pale, though, it's clear there's nothing on his mind except you. In a good way.

His hands

Wriggling, stuffed in his pockets, wildly waving...he left all that gesturing behind with other human frailties. Your dark dude is different: he has to remember to fidget to look human. Otherwise he could make a fortune as one of those living statues (and *really* start creeping people out).

Hands hanging loose by his sides show he's chilled, and, of course, an arm slung casually around your shoulders is always welcome...from the right boy.

His body

Is he facing you? A sure sign of an honest boy is one whose movements are fluid and open. Vamps are always pretty preoccupied (it's that sensory overload they have to deal with), but a relaxed stance tells you that you've not hit Perilsville yet!

Enjoy the moment: when you chose each other, you signed up to some uncanny undercurrents that you wouldn't have got with the captain of the football team, so, when he's relaxed, you can relish calm karma even more with your vamp.

The full picture

Take a step back. Eyes pale and soft, not staring; hands reaching toward you and eager for a hug; body turned into you, open and relaxed. The omens are good: enjoy your date.

Reading your Vamp's Body Language II

What's not!

His eyes

When he looks at you, his eyes should be light and soft. The darker and more fixed they are, the more cautious you should be. Never forget that however much he's into you, a boy's gotta eat! If he's staring hard and his eyes have turned dark, you've crossed the line from love interest to entrée, and it's time to go.

His hands

Your vamp'll never be one for big gestures, but if his laidback lean turns into something more tense, this is not a good sign: think panther getting ready to spring. Stiff shoulders aren't a good thing either: he may be about to fall into the predator's crouch. If the eyes didn't alert you, let's say it again. It's time to go. Now.

His body

It's always icy cool, but now it's tense and tight too. Read our lips. It's time to *go*!

The full picture

Don't hang around to analyse the signs in detail, because it may be the last thing you do.

THE COMMON FACTOR

....

Vamp-boys have one thing in common with
the human type: when he looks shifty—
whatever bit of the body's sending the
message—the words "i'll call you" will
carry no weight.

What's it telling you? Not to waste your
time. Chalk him up to experience and find
a guy worth working your magic on.

To Vamp or Not to Vamp?

That is the question… Drawn by his electric magnetism and killer style, you picked a vamp for a reason. Now you've been out once or twice, make a cool-headed comparison on how he stacks up against your merely human dates.

High-School Honey

Pros

➤ It doesn't take a psychic to guess what he's thinking.

➤ When he's thirsty, a glass of H_2O does the job.

➤ He asks (needs) your advice when shopping for clothes.

➤ You share the same interests (well, mostly).

➤ You usually have fun when you're together…

Cons

➤ He hasn't a clue what's on *your* mind.

➤ His manners can be a bit, uh, basic.

➤ He can't coordinate an outfit to save his life.

➤ He keeps the TV eternally tuned to the sports channel.

➤ …but he can be really juvenile with his mates.

High-School Honey

Gorgeous Vamp-Boy

Gorgeous Vamp-Boy

Pros

- Hello? Supernatural powers?!

- His killer cool has worked wonders for your image.

- He notices how you look and what you're wearing.

- Mind his manners? He's a bona fide gent!

- His intensity thrills you, and you always feel safe with him…

Cons

- You can't keep a secret from him. Ever.

- He has more style than you do!

- He doesn't sleep. Just watches while you do.

- He doesn't eat, so doing dinner's not much fun.

- …except when he's thirsty.

THE VERDICT?

You chose the bad guy, didn't you? With all his drawbacks, your seasoned vamp makes warm-blooded boys seem a little…immature.

Meeting the Friends

The first time you're invited out with your new crush's friends is definitely big news! But you'd be forgiven a flutter of nerves when he suggests a double date with his more immortal mates. So how to play it?

Follow our brief guide to getting in with the crowd (and home in one piece)!

Do

★ Give yourself the once over. Okay, they've got centuries of accumulated chic, but you can see in a mirror! Keep the blusher to a minimum, though. You don't want to remind everyone that you're the only person there with fully functional circulation.

★ Act cheerful and confident, even if you feel nervous. When you're in daunting company (human or otherwise), faking confidence is the best way to get a supply of the real thing.

★ Speak up! Vamps tend to stick together, so you'll be a novelty to his friends. Let them know you have feelings and opinions too. Although you may be an unusual addition to the group, you're his girl, not his pet.

★ Check you're not wearing anything that could worry a vampire. You probably don't have holy water on you, but it's easy to forget a little crucifix around your neck. (You could always slip it in your purse, though—just in case.)

Don't

★ Suggest anything competitive.
An evening's bowling might be
a fun night out for your warm-
blooded gang, but in supernatural
company you'll end up a sore
loser. A gig, a movie, or hitting the
dancefloor would all be better
choices. Vamps are super-
graceful, though, so have your
best moves ready!

★ Ask too many questions.
Vampires are sensitive about their
lifestyle, and you don't want to be
taken for just another thrill-seeker.

★ Forget to eat before you go. And
you'd better hope that he and his
posse have already fed, too!

Living Up to the Undead Image

Back when you were dating ordinary boys, you used to wish they'd lose all those crimes against fashion they called clothes. Guess what? Now you've got a vampire in tow, you find that you're in the style hot seat.

When you're having to look to your laurels as you step out with your fella, here's how to enjoy it.

Made to match

You don't catch a vampire making a huge effort to look right—one of his charms is that this guy looks great without even trying. Match his nonchalance and don't freak out—it was your natural beauty he fancied first, so trying too hard might be going backward!

Enhance your everyday image instead. You can have the same fun with fashion that you always did, and charm your new boy into the bargain. Turning clothes into hard work is guaranteed to take all the pleasure out of them, so keep it casual.

Devil in the detail

Fashion doesn't have to cost a fortune! Whether it's a costume party or another day at school, whatever outfit your vamp picks, with his keen eye for detail he'll pull it off beautifully. Take a leaf from his book and learn those little tricks, from belts to badges, that keep your dress-up dynamic and your clothes current.

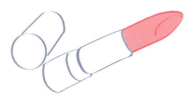

Making up…

…is hard to do. Or at least it is when you want your makeup to work with his paler-than-pale looks. But don't forget that one of the reasons he likes you is that your skin and expression change with your moods (unlike the permanently perfect vamp complexion).

Don't go dead-white gothic just to match him. A bit of blusher or foundation teamed with smoky eyes should do the trick. Maybe steer clear of the blood-red lipstick, though.

The Vampire Diaries I

You've found your vampire, you've been on a couple of dates, and you're starting to get in with his gang. So how's it going? Calm and cool, or hot and bothered? These pages are your personal romance record.

Where we met

....

....

....

....

....

What he said

....

....

....

....

....

How he looked

....

....

....

....

....

First date

....

....

....

....

....

How I feel

....

....

....

....

....

Getting Close

You met him, you netted him, and he's dead keen (literally). But you've still got an awful lot to learn about your drop-dead gorgeous killer-crush. This chapter is all the study buddy you need.

Sweep him off his feet with the hottest spots to hang out. Plus brush up on the latest vamp lore (some is dusty old legend, but there are a few nuggets of truth); the greatest vampire movies of all time; and where to draw the line with a boy who knows literally all about you...

Hotting Up or Cooling Off?

Is he really into you? Or are his feelings as cool as his whiter-shade-of-pale complexion? If you find your vamp's behavior baffling, check your dating data to find out whether he's white-hot with passion or icy with indifference.

→ What he does	→ What it means
❧ He's distracted—constantly charming, but here, there, and everywhere!	❧ The attraction's so strong, he's not completely sure he's got it under control.
❧ Sometimes you can feel him watching you as though he's learning you by heart.	❧ He's captivated, and his feelings are growing as he finds out more about you.
❧ When you go out, he only has eyes for you; other days, there are other girls.	❧ His laser gaze conceals a roving eye; this vamp finds safety by dating in numbers.
❧ You cross paths in class, and he's always friendly; you've been out once or twice.	❧ He likes and feels relaxed around you.
❧ He's a semi-stalker, but not much of a talker—he seems to want to get you alone.	❧ Nothing good. He's acting like a predator, not a date.

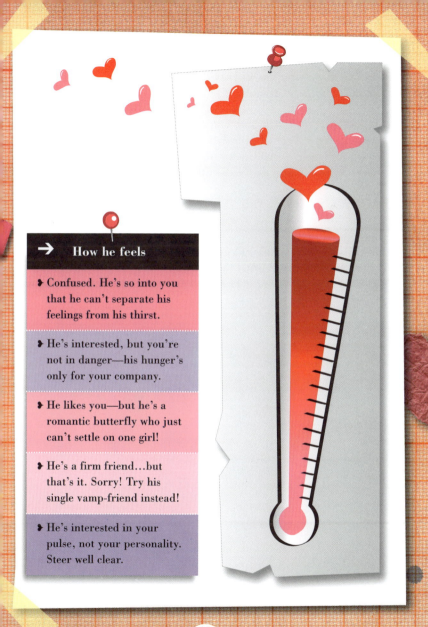

Undead Dates I

He's hardly your sun, sea, and surf kind of guy, but the idea of going for a Type-O milkshake doesn't really appeal either. So what do you do with your vamp boy that doesn't involve bright lights, maiming, or the apocalypse?

Definitely do's!

The movie theater

The ultimate date location: it's dark, it's discreet, and it guarantees at least two hours with the man of your dreams. Perfect for avoiding those awkward moments when you run out of things to say, but take him to see *Twilight* and he'll have to get the message.

Laser tag

You've bagged yourself a boy with extrasensory perception, cobra-like reflexes, night vision, and the body of a god! How could you lose?! Running around in the dark is great fun, and won't scorch his skin like sunlight can. Just don't let him actually fly. That's cheating.

Eat meat!

However veggie you may be, you'll have to face up to the fact that this guy has a major iron deficiency. Whether you go for a slap-up steak or a burger from the next-door diner, he might not have much of an appetite for human food, but he'll thank you for thinking of him.

The carnival

Step right up! What better place to put your boy's superskills to good use than at a fair? With his extra-sharp vision he's sure to win you something from one of the stalls. Okay, so a goldfish in a bag isn't the first  thing on your mind on a date, but with the lights, party atmosphere, and the ferris wheel to snuggle up on, you might just win his heart as well.

Gig date

If music be the food of love, rock out! Nothing gets rid of your troubles, whether you're 16 or 160, like throwing yourself about to guitars cranked up to 11. Seeing a band you both like, or discovering a new one together, is something you can share and is a great bonding experience.

Outdoor adventure

The call of the wild's hard to resist, and not just for vampires! If you're the outdoor type, let your hair down and blow off some steam with a day (or two) at an outdoor adventure center. There should be somewhere in your area that offers activities like abseiling or tree-climbing—plus the leafy canopy will ensure the sun can't damage his sensitive skin or (worst case scenario) reduce him to a pile of dust!

Undead Dates II

Die a date death!

The beach

Come on, you weren't seriously thinking of catching rays with a fella so pale he practically reflects light? He'd be all for helping you apply the Factor 30, but he can't share in any of the fun.

Take a seat in the shade and watch the world go by. Or, even better, get together to watch the sunset. After all, he's not the only one who should look after their skin—it's safer for you, too!

Jewelry store

Taking a guy anywhere near a selection of large diamond rings tends to be a recipe for disaster, but when there are discreet crosses and bling crucifixes on every stand, your boy isn't going to thank you—crosses are kryptonite to a vamp. Stick to charm bracelets.

Smoothie bar

Juices and smoothies are a fabulous way to stay in shape and feel great, but you'll have to accept that he'll never be a big fruit fan. If you're really craving Vitamin C or some comfort superfoods, there's no harm in swinging by—but get one to go.

The zoo

Suss this one out first. Your vamp-boy might have tamed his inner beast, but he's still a free spirit at heart. He won't appreciate seeing animals locked up and put on parade, plus there's always a chance his nocturnal nature might get the better of him in the bat enclosure!

French cuisine

Ah, *l'amour*! It's true that France is the country of romance, and a cozy candlelit evening for two might seem the perfect way to recreate that continental feeling. But steer clear of the food!

Not only will your date remain indifferent to everything but meat served unappetizingly bloody but garlic breath is a passion killer whoever you're with, and vamps hate the stuff, which means you're guaranteed to go home without a goodnight kiss. Is it so bad that snails are off the menu?

Shopping

With hundreds of years under his belt, your vampire honey has probably learned a little patience by now. But when it comes to a woman on a mission to *shop*, don't be deceived. No man, alive or dead, enjoys waiting around changing rooms for hours on end.

Don't despair! When it comes to vintage shopping, a vampire will shine. Ditch the department stores for the fleamarkets, and give him a chance to show off. Who knows? You might get more than you bargained for!

Vampire vs. Friends

You've met his friends—now it's time to return the favor. And although he's a one-to-one talker second to none, you're worried how he'll play to the warm-blooded crowd on a normal date night. Here's how to smooth his way and ensure that he's as popular with the living as he is with the undead.

Part of the crowd

Do

★ Pick an evening date. He'll find it easier to mix once the sun's gone down. And his pallor will be less noticeable after dark.

★ Let him know the dress code. The only fault with vamp style is that it's sometimes a little formal. Gorgeous though he looks in full vintage, it may not sit well at a ballgame.

★ Let him do his own mingling. Once he's at ease and settled into the group, move around yourself. If he needs you, he can track you faster than any other guy in the room.

★ Introduce him. Incredibly, most vanilla vamps (that's the veggie kind) are quite shy in regular human company, so play the hostess just as you would with any friend from out of town.

★ Suggest a venue where he won't stand out. Movies or a concert will work well; an evening playing team sports or a meal out won't.

Out in the cold

Don't

★ Show off. However tempting it is to persuade your guy to demonstrate his superskills, you'll embarrass him. Like most boys, he'd really rather fit in with the crowd. Keep his flying displays as a secret between the two of you.

★ Stress. It's natural to feel nervous the first time you bring new blood to meet your buddies, but if you just act natural, people are more likely to accept your date without comment—even if he does look like a rock star and dance like a diva.

★ Let the group flirt loose on him. He's *your* date! Plus you don't want him developing a sudden thirst, now do you? Even if he has got iron self-control.

Quiz: Hot Girl for a Cool Guy

They're the coolest guys on earth (not having a pulse will do that to you), so how can you persuade a vamp that you're the hottest girl for him? His supersenses are always on red-alert, so catching his attention may be a challenge, but follow your natural style and you'll soon melt his icy cool. Just pick the options you think are most like you for failsafe tips to catch your boy's golden eye.

1 It's Friday night; what's your preferred date destination?

a. The movies—something old-style and romantic. ☆

b. Going bowling—you love that retro vibe. ☆

c. A night under canvas, getting close to nature. ☆

d. Out clubbing till the small hours—why waste time sleeping? ☆

2 What will you wear?

a. A great little dress you found in a one-off store this afternoon. ☆

b. Your favorite online buys: cute vintage shirt and skirt. ☆

c. Jeans, sneakers, and a good thick sweater. ☆

d. You're into goth at the moment: black and black, with some black accents. ☆

3 What will you talk about?

a. You'll let him lead the conversation. ☆

b. You'll be keeping it light. It's more fun kidding around. ☆

c. Green issues—you're always looking for converts to the cause. ☆

d. You'll let your moves do the talking. There's no need for conversation when you can dance. ☆

4 At dinner, what's on your menu?

a. Fine dining at a chic restaurant. ☆

b. A burger, eaten on the move. ☆

c. The vegetarian option, cooked on an open fire. ☆

d. A snack in the small hours from the boho café only you two know about. ☆

5 Your fantasy weekend break would be:

a. A new city—plenty of art galleries and cool cafés. ☆

b. Something fun and unexpected—maybe a course in salsa or surfing. ☆

c. Volunteering on an urban gardens project. ☆

d. A summer festival, featuring all the best bands. ☆

6 What would be the best impulse gift your boy could buy you?

a. A full day's luxury at the best spa in town. ☆

b. An afternoon white-water rafting. ☆

c. A trip to visit an endangered species—in its home habitat. ☆

d. His 'n' hers tattoos of his own design. ☆

Answers: Hot Girl for a Cool Guy

Mostly As

Your sophisticated outlook means you're made for the older guy hidden inside a vamp-boy's eternally teenage exterior. Plus your love of the good things in life lets him show off the debonair airs he's picked up down the decades. Play up your feminine side—it'll bring out the alpha in him—and do take charge occasionally. Even if he's been around for centuries, you can still teach him a thing or two!

Mostly Bs

With your upbeat and action-packed attitude, you'll make a good pair with the guy who never sleeps. Even though you both know that he can surf without a board (and fly without a plane…), he'll enjoy your efforts to keep up with his supercharged pace.

Classy Crush

Nonstop Hottie

Mostly Cs

Opposites attract! Your green-loving credentials may baffle your boy, but he shares your love of nature, so you should have some good times outdoors. You love his nonexistent carbon footprint (he doesn't need heat, he can see in the dark, and he likes his food very fresh). Relish your differences—just don't expect to convert him from his carnivorous ways.

Mostly Ds

With your eclectic approach and too-cool-for-school image, you're a natural to attract an undead date. Your boy will appreciate your late-night lifestyle and innovative ideas, even if he hacked into your mental hard drive and heard them long before they came out of your mouth. And you can act as a reflection of his own image— useful when he's never got to grips with mirrors.

Eco-Warrior

Dark 'n' Handsome

Vital Vamp Facts

Bram Stoker, creator of the original Dracula, started a lot of those vicious vamp rumors that give them such a bad rep, but they've got almost nothing in common with the cool 'n' collected contemporary vampire. What with those dusty old tomes and some very misleading movies, it's not surprising that you're not sure what's true or false when the real deal hits.

Here's a short myth-buster of the most common legends, so that you don't put your human foot in it during your first few weeks together.

Sunburn

The tiniest ray of sunshine will reduce a vampire to dust.

True or false? Uh, no. Vampires are naturally drawn to cool, dark places, but they can withstand the sun. It makes them feel noticeable, though (some vamps light up like a Christmas tree on a sunny day), so they tend to avoid it. Don't count on too many fine-day dates.

Lazy bones

During daylight hours he naps in a coffin.

True or false? Oh, please… The guy is regularly in school, he makes the highest grades, and have you ever seen him getting creased or dirty? Plus he doesn't even seem to need sleep. No, this one's pure myth.

Weak spots

Hold vampires at bay with garlic or crucifixes. And the only way to despatch the undead is a stake through the heart—this may have started with Stoker, but Buffy did a lot to keep it current.

True or false? Well. He certainly hates garlic—but then so does anyone who's hit garlic breath as they close in for a clinch. Crucifixes are a real aversion, although it's more aesthetic than life-threatening. As for stakes through the heart? Who wouldn't be destroyed by them? So maybe aim to eat garlic only on school nights, and ignore the morbid stake stuff. Even if it's in the textbooks, you're aiming for a happy-ever-after, not ending up like Romeo and Juliet.

Dress-up Drac

He's always impeccably and formally dressed, with slicked-back hair and an opera cape.

True or false? The immaculate part tends to be true, even with modern vamps, but he's more likely to be sporting a cutting-edge quiff than a creepy-uncle combover!

Red eye

His eyes darken when he smells blood.

True or false? Yes, his eyes turn from pale to deep black or red when he's worked up. If you're ever worried that his focus is becoming a little too intense, sneak a peek at his peepers. You'll know straightaway.

Must-See Movies

Now that you've exploded a few vamp myths, you can snigger (and snuggle) along with your squeeze watching the ridiculous mistakes movies have made about vampires time and again. Here we have nearly a century's worth of greats to choose from, although your date may well have seen some of these first time around.

Here's a top ten: some silly, some scary, and some strictly cult material for indie flick chicks only.

1 Twilight (2008), New Moon (2009)

As if you needed telling! Far more accurate than most vamp movie stories, as well as being killer romantic. And there are four in the series, so there's more to look forward to.

2 Underworld (2003)

Very scary, and maybe a bit gruesome (ask your vamp if it's right for you!), but this has the bonus of putting both vampires and werewolves in the same neighborhood.

3 Blood: The Lost Vampire (2000)

Lovely manga saga, although sadly uninformed on vampire habits and lifestyle. You'll really enjoy it for the fabulous cartoon vamps.

4 The Little Vampire (2000)

Showing the sweeter side of vamps, this is a cute kids' classic about a vamp befriending a human. Sound familiar?

5 Interview with the Vampire (1994)

Featuring Brad Pitt as a vamp who's struggling (none-too-successfully) to stay vegetarian. Moody and magnetic, and that's just the lighting effects.

6 Buffy the Vampire Slayer (1992)

Long before the TV series came the movie. This is still the one that most vamps credit with modernizing their image, although plenty of the old myths still put in an appearance.

7 Innocent Blood (1992)

Another vamp with a conscience, but this time she's female. Dark, dramatic, and very gripping; plenty of excuses here for burying your face in your date's shoulder!

8 Blood for Dracula (1974)

Also known as the "Pop-Art Dracula," this one was promoted by top Pop artist Andy Warhol and features one of the coolest casts ever seen in a vampire movie. They're almost good-looking enough to compete with the real thing. Again, check it's not too scary before you get started.

And finally, a couple of real oldies:

9 Dracula (1931)

The original Dracula legend, complete with a suave, blood-drinking count and plenty of shrieking, swooning victims.

10 Nosferatu (1922)

A silent classic, with a less-than-gorgeous ghoul at the heart of it. Nothing to do with the real vampire you know and love, but genuinely creepy if you're a fan of cult classics.

That's Private!

As you get to know him better, you'll learn pretty fast that your fella's a mind reader—and that means much more than him picking out the perfect birthday gift. But while vamps find it quite natural, it's tough when you're human and can't return the favor.

If you feel invaded by his constant mental presence, here are some tactics to guard your psychic privacy:

Ask!

It's maybe never occurred to your boy that you don't always want your mind read. After all, it's one of his everyday skills (and he's used to his peers popping in and out of his psyche). So before you get uptight about his hotwiring your thoughts, try the logical solution: tell him you simply don't like it.

If he doesn't understand straight off, explain that it's a bit like someone clocking your personal texts or e-mails. You're not being secretive; like any girl, you simply need a little privacy.

Meditation

He'll soon get bored if there's nothing to read! Vamps are baffled by meditation, and your boy, faced by a Zen-induced blank slate, will go and bother someone else's consciousness. Plus it's a great stress-reliever for you. Slip into a leotard, fold into the lotus pose, and "Ommmmm…"

Gossip girl

Teen vamps are boys too! And their tolerance for girly gossip is just as low as any other teenage boy's. Run through a long conversation with your best friend in your head. Include all the details that boys are most bored by: a recent girly gathering, what everyone was wearing, where you went (several hours at the mall), what you bought… Now just play it on a mental loop. Before long, he'll be testing his mind-reading skills elsewhere, and you can keep your secrets in peace.

Vamp Dating: Hot or Not?

Before you fill in your progress on the next page, go through the pros and cons of dating your vamp. What do you love? What's a major turn-off? Back in Chapter 1, you compared your vamp with a regular boy; this time you're just checking him out for what he is.

Hot: the things you love

❥ His manners are old-school; he's got acres more class than the other cavemen you've dated.

❥ He's a fab talker—smart and sensitive. And he knows how to share a silence, too.

❥ His looks—he's beautiful. This may not be number one on your list, but you could look at him just as long as you could listen to him talk.

❥ You get to share his superpowers—you reap the benefits of his batlike hearing, his hawklike vision, and his bearlike strength. Suddenly you know how it feels to have a superhero all to yourself!

Not: the things you don't

❥ Since he can tell what you're thinking, you're always a few mental steps behind.

❥ He's totally danger-blind. You know his reflexes are superfast, but crossing the road with him is still a pretty scary experience.

❥ Your mom loves him. She's hated all your previous dates, yet she goes starry eyed when your vampire calls. It's unnatural…and just a bit creepy.

❥ You have to stay sensible around him. You can't ever be really silly because you need to keep your wits about you. He's given you a crash course in growing up and it's not all a bed of roses.

THE VERDICT?

So, how are you feeling? Still drawn to his magnetism? Or feeling a little eclipsed by his powerful persona?

The Vampire Diaries II

You're getting closer, and his supernatural night skills don't make you so nervous. You've learned what makes a good day, or night, out for both of you, and what's best avoided—you won't be repeating the evening at that French bistro any time soon! Suss out how it's going and decide whether your vamp is headed for official VB (Vamp-Boyfriend) status.

What I like best about him

....

....

....

....

....

What (I think!) he likes best about me

....

....

....

....

....

Things I'd still like to know about him

....

....

....

....

....

Our best date so far

....

....

....

....

....

How I feel

....

....

....

....

....

3

Going Steady

Your dates are getting regular (fangtastic!),
you've met his friends (awesome!) and he's met
yours (well, it went okay...) — and it dawns on
you...you're going steady! Here's how to keep that
tight-knit, joined-at-the-hip quality while still
giving yourselves a bit of breathing space.

We've got ways to chill together, and how to moan
about your vamp just as if he were a regular guy.
Swot up on the undead universe, learn to capture
his classic vampire style, and find out what your
squeeze really thinks about dating you.

Hang with the Fanged I

Your very first dates were probably as fraught as your "does-he-really-like-me?" fears could make them. Now that you're less frantic, keep your twosome fresh by trying out some new things.

Some great ideas to try...

Ghostbusting

If you fancy heading out ghost-hunting, who better to come along than your fella? His laser eyes can spot all manner of spooks, and he's surely the ultimate protection against dark forces. You might even want to make some extra cash by starting up a ghost tour together. With a real vampire on board, everyone's going to want to sign up for the creepiest option in your neighborhood.

Eco-volunteering

Eco interests are one area where human and vampire interests meet. He's all for the environment. After all, if the wilderness dies out, where's he going to do his big-game hunting? And you want to reduce your carbon impact, too.

Whether you live in city, town or in the country, there are always loads of green causes to shout about, from saving the whale to responsible recycling. Take your pick from a huge range of options and enjoy doing some good for the planet together...

Hiking trip

Head out into the wildest wilderness you can find and enjoy some alone time together. He can hunt for his food while you forage for yours—and while you may prefer not to share actual meals, you're bound to get close around the campfire afterward. Plus, with a seasoned hunter at hand, wave good-bye to worries about bears or other large predators ruining the moment.

Circus skills workshop

The newest fitness fad for city-dwellers (though probably harder to find if you live out of town), circus workshops challenge your fitness levels and your balance. Plus they're beyond trendy.

If you're a little nervous, what better companion for high-wire or trapeze training than someone who is always absolutely ready 'n' able to catch you, should you fall? This may, too, be one of the very few leisure activities where your vamp's superspeed and ultra-flexibility may pass almost unnoticed among normal folk.

Hang with the Fanged II

...And some to scrap

Volunteering

We know we've only just suggested going all-out for eco causes on the previous pages, but there's one area of volunteering it's best to avoid: no hospital needs a vamp on the wards, especially when the blood wagon comes around asking for donations.

Cooking classes

A fun option for some couples—learning a new cuisine together. Yummy! But be careful which you pick. The sushi and sashimi class will probably be safe enough, but keep away from the authentic Texas barbecue course—raw meat will work your vamp up and turn your pickier palate. Eugh! Who wants to learn how to handle a side of beef anyway? Sounds like one for the good ol' boys back at the ranch, not the average vamp.

Horse-riding

Horses and immortals don't go, full stop. Horses are sensitive to vampire vibes, and riding astride a panicky pony is one of the few physical activities that your mate won't excel at.

If you're keen on trekking or eventing, keep it for the times when your fella is off pursuing his own interests elsewhere and go with your horse-mad girlfriend.

Hot tubbing

If there's one in your or a friend's back garden, it can seem the perfect place for a teen couple to unwind together. But you're not the average couple. Hot water and jets warm you up—and may make your naturally enticing scent too tempting to your still-chilled boy's sensitive nose. Suddenly he'll be lusting after your blood rather than your body. This is an option that's best avoided.

Major Moans

You're crazy about him…but sometimes he drives you nuts!
Prep for a discreet dissing session with your BFF with these
pointy problems—plus a few gripes your guy won't give you.

He drives you mad when he…

➤ Reads your mind. This is instinctive to most vamps. He can't help it.

➤ Comes top of the class. You're proud of him, but when he's first every time, it sometimes gets you down. Just think how good your grades'd be after a century.

➤ Smells you. You love that he likes your scent, but sometimes it feels like you're fielding a faithful pooch. And you never, ever want to hear the words, "You smell good enough to eat!" from this boy.

➤ Won't hang with your gang. Leave him be—most vamps need as much downtime as Greta Garbo. At least you're not one of those creepy couples who always come as a pair.

At least he doesn't…

➤ Love toilet humor. Your human dates may have found farts, smelly feet, and other gross-out stuff funny, but your vamp outgrew this phase centuries ago.

➤ Act awkward around your parents. Most vamps will charm the pants off Mom and Dad.

➤ Look a mess. He's learned that cleanliness is next to…well, maybe not godliness, but he knows it's popular with girls. You'll definitely have no BO bother with a vampire.

➤ Leave you to walk home alone. There's no one more safety conscious—he'll see you to your door *and* watch over you while you sleep.

Subzero: Looking as Cool as your Guy

It's no bad thing that all those undead years have left your boy with a spot-on sense of style. But any girl would sigh a bit at being shown up by her guy every time.

Want to match up? Try these tips:

Work a look

Even when he's going for shabby chic, his jeans are torn in all the right places and his battered old jacket hangs just so. If you want to equal him, make sure that you're style-consistent.

Whatever look you pick, try to follow it through from head to toe, whether it's preppy or cowgirl. You don't have to look as though you're off to a costume party—just pay attention to the detail.

Emo/goth

The classic vamp look—the one that lures girls with its bad-boy image —is dark and dangerous. If you want to try it, you could go goth (or its younger style sister emo) every so often, even if it's streets away from your regular choices. This is a look that hasn't really been beaten since the 1980s and punk, so look out old fashion and music zines for ideas…

Authenticity

Vamps often love fashions from when they were young first time around. Now that you're close, take a look at his style signals. Leaning towards a sharp jacket? 1920s maybe. Bold patterns? Could be the 1960s—or even the 1860s great age of the dandy.

Maybe you're close enough now for him to have revealed his original birth date. Once you know, you could try couple-dressing occasionally. He shines at the vintage store, so let your imaginations loose and go for a full period look—just for fun.

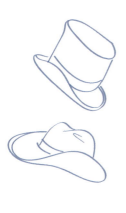

AVOID!

Even if you think you'd enjoy it, resist the temptation to dress up as a vamp victim— the classic Hollywood fang-fodder. That flowing hair, floating white dress, and uber-innocent look may raise undesirable impulses in your boy.

Vamp Online

How do you hack into the 21st-century vamp-boy's brain?
His computer habits are bound to give you one or two clues
about his character. Does he...

Blog?

If your boy's a keen blogger, chances are you've landed the PR man of
your local coven. A micro-manager who likes everything just so, his blog
tells you how he wants the world to see him (and generally they oblige).
If you can get behind the managed and confident façade, you'll find this
boy longs for someone he can open up to.

Social network?

Does he use Facebook to keep up with human pals (and Fangbook for vamp friends)? DJ of the information superhighway, this boy's main aim is to show everyone a good time. His surfing habits confirm what you already know: that what you see is what you get. He doesn't worry about his image too much, so long as he's got plenty of fun to look forward to when he gets to the next big party.

IM?

Instant messaging has loads of benefits. You can chat late into the night (okay, he doesn't need to sleep, but you have curfew), sometimes it's nice to talk at a slight distance (especially if he looked hungry when you saw him earlier), and there's something thrilling about seeing each new line ping up on the screen. Just one thing: check that you're the only girl getting the benefit of his late-night virtual flirting technique—if he's not there in person, it's a lot easier for him to play away…

Send undead e-mails?

He favors one-to-ones over Facebook but keeps up with a vast range of people—vamps, humans, and even werewolves—all over the world. He's the first to know everyone's news, and is the guy they rely on to have his finger on the pulse (metaphorically speaking). He's amazingly warm-hearted for a vamp, and if you want him, he'll be yours for keeps.

Quiz: A Vamp's View

Now that you've bonded big-time, look at your love through vampire eyes. Get him to take our quiz to see the goings on in that handsome head, and find out whether you've got a fanged flirtation or long-term love.

1 What do you like best about her?

a. Her smile. It reflects her warmth and sparkle. ☆

b. Her eyes. They're a gorgeous change from gold or red. ☆

c. Her bod. She's the fittest human you've ever met. ☆

d. Her skin. Her blushes remind you that she's 100% girl, 0% vamp. ☆

2 And if you had to find fault, what would her downside be?

a. Nothing. She's pretty cute, even when she can't keep up. ☆

b. Even your special insight doesn't always tell you what's on her mind. ☆

c. She's a laugh a minute, but rarely shows her serious side. ☆

d. You don't know if she's keen on you, or your bad-boy rep. ☆

3 You can spend a date any way you choose. Which would you pick?

a. One-on-one, just talking. You could talk to her for eternity. ☆

b. You'd let her choose; you want to find out what she likes. ☆

c. Poker evening. Psychic powers mean a sure win. ☆

d. A vamp-powered flight together. She'll love the thrill! ☆

4 You got her home after curfew, and her dad's grounded her. What will she do?

a. Enlist you in convincing Dad that you're a responsible couple. ☆

b. Patiently wait out the punishment. ☆

c. Climb out her window for an illicit adventure with you. ☆

d. Persuade you to fly in her window and keep her company. ☆

5 Where do you like to step out together?

a. Out in the country; you don't care about the local hotspots. ☆

b. A quiet corner in the local coffee shop. ☆

c. At the mall, where she can show you off to all her friends. ☆

d. Dancing. The later, flashier, and more fashionable the venue, the better. ☆

6 Do you think she enjoys dating a vampire? If so, why?

a. She loves dating you, pure and simple. The vampire bit's just a bonus! ☆

b. She dates you, doesn't she? Actions speak louder than words. ☆

c. She's a full-time fun-lover and she likes your lively side. ☆

d. She's thrilled by the novelty; she'll try anything once. ☆

Answers: A Vamp's View

Mostly As

You feel so strongly about her that it's almost…human. Such a loved-up couple shouldn't have many worries on the romantic front; both of you are concentrating on the big pluses in your partnership and neither of you wants to explore your darker side. You accept each other's limitations, too, so you're unlikely to get frustrated with her earthbound qualities, and she won't nag you about your cold-blooded habits. This one could be a keeper.

Mostly Bs

You're keen; she's less certain. You love the enigma that surrounds her—human girls are pretty exotic: so soft and changeable after the vamp variety! She's intriguingly sensitive and you can't see through her as you can with most humans. Even though you have a century or two on her technical age, she's an old soul in a beguilingly youthful bod. But be cautious—although you're the carnivore in this relationship, you're still the one who may end up getting hurt!

Mostly Cs

You've landed the original good-time girl: a nonstop, all-singing, all-dancing date who embraces your differences (she's even been known to use your perma-cold skin as an instant ice pack on an ankle sprain after an action-packed evening). Is she after a long-term (or even eternal) vamp liaison, though? That's not so sure.

Mostly Ds

You're both full-on into your relationship, but watch out! It's clear that she loves the vamp vibe but your answers are just a little ambiguous. Have you got your primal nature well under control? She never forgets you're a vamp, and you never forget she's a (deliciously warm-blooded) girl—but neither of you worry about the full implications of that. Dice with danger if you want, but make sure it doesn't end in tears.

Killing Time: Vampire Hobbies

Now that your relationship's as stable as it can be with a guy who can fly, you should share more of life than just dates— why not hobbies, too?

Here are a few faves he may go for:

Turn back time

Nostalgia is another characteristic of the immortals. It's because his childhood seems (is...) so distant that you'll sometimes find your guy carrying on like your granny about long-gone pleasures. When he's in serious need of an under-10 fix, try something simple and uncomplicated: kite-flying, maybe, or building a sandcastle, so have fun rediscovering your own childish side.

Shadow chasing

A sort of undead hide-and-seek that only vamps are fast enough to play. It's a bit of an in-joke—shadows, like reflections, aren't assets that vamps have—but he'd love you to come along and share in it. Indulge him, and he'll be putty in your hands.

Photography

He loves his darkroom, even though he won't feature in any of the photos. Still, if he's on the snapping side of the camera, it hardly matters.

Vampires usually prefer to work with old-style film rather than digitally, although with his natural dexterity he'll be a Photoshop pro. Spend a day taking shots—you can be his model and his muse.

Reenactment societies

You may not really have seen the social side of your boyfriend except with his undead pals. So his sloping off to those authentic historical reenactment societies may come as a surprise.

Given that he may have been at Culloden, Wounded Knee, or Iwo Jima first time around, though, it's not hard to spot the source of his interest. And you can go along with it, clad in various forms of bonnet or corset, according to date, and watch him enjoy playing dress up.

Parkour

This is basically the art of not-touching-the-floor. Parkour, also known as free-running, involves tackling a town- or country-scape, going over, rather than around, any obstacles. Vamps adore it, and it's good for you, too, so long as you're feeling fairly fit and reasonably brave.

Of course, parkouring with the undead is great—he's ready to save you if you put a foot wrong, so you can be as daring as you like. Five stars for fitness, fun, and bonding.

Meet the family

Vamps are made, not born, and becoming immortal gives them a real feel for their roots. If he suggests spending an hour or two online or in the library trying to trace his fanged forebears, go for it, even if it sounds a bit tame. If you've ever wondered about his background (Venetian palazzo? Western ranch? Transylvanian castle?), this date's a shortcut to finding out much more about him.

Sudoku

The closet geeky side of your vamp shines through with his number-crunching. He's a natural at sudoku and he'll also take on quite complex conundrums purely for fun. Unless you're a math whiz yourself, you may be a little less hooked on this hobby, but stick with it—at the very least it'll help to improve your grades in class!

DON'T GO

★ Hunting. After all this time he's unlikely to hit on you in a carnivorous way, but watching him tuck in won't be pretty—and you certainly won't feel like kissing him afterward.

★ Also a no-no—the tattoo parlor. Okay, the guy has iron(-deficient) control, but this place is enough to turn your stomach and rouse his appetite.

Vamp History 101

Well, it's only polite to learn a bit about his culture. We've done a little homework on a handful of the biggest vampires in history—in real life and legend!

Vlad III, Prince of Wallachia

The inspiration for Count Dracula, and the start of many vampire myths. Vlad lived in the 15th century, and is the best-known figure from vamp history. Fabled for his bravery but also his cruelty, he lived in what is now part of Romania. The whole Transylvanian blood-drinking thing starts here.

Gilles de Rais

A suave French vampire. Like Vlad, he lived in the 15th century, and fought alongside Joan of Arc, becoming a military and national hero before rumors of his "alternative" lifestyle were leaked. Just as Vlad was the model for Dracula, Gilles is believed to be the source for the legendary Bluebeard and his roomful of murdered wives. Icky.

Countess Elizabeth Bathory

Around a century after Vlad and Gilles, Elizabeth, a Hungarian noblewoman, is vampire history's femme fatale. She was believed not just to drink blood but to bathe in it, too, to maintain her icy beauty. Most families have at least one embarrassing relative—Elizabeth is definitely the skeleton in the respectable vampire closet.

Count Dracula

Not the first, and fictional rather than real, but Bram Stoker's Dracula, from the 1897 book, is the most famous vamp of all, with his transformative powers, his nocturnal coffin naps, and his constant, unquenchable thirst. Vampires have mixed feelings about Dracula, though. Some veggie vamps think he's ruined their rep, but most have to admit that, good or bad, Stoker did a lot to put vamps on the map.

Revision Session

Look back on what you *thought* you knew about him before you dated, and what you know for sure now you're official. It might surprise you!

What you thought then

- Humans and vampires don't mix. However gorgeous he is, I can't date him—I'd never survive it!

- He's as hard as iron and as cold as ice—all instinct, but no heart.

- He'd want to change me, even if he likes me as a person. He'll need to turn me into a vampire before we can date.

- Humans bore him. He'll get impatient with how I can't keep up.

- Vampires are governed by whole sets of rules that I don't understand—stuff to do with coffins, garlic, stakes, and crucifixes.

What you know now

- A human/vamp couple *can* work—but you need to be super-patient to handle his supernatural status.

- Vamps have feelings like the rest of us, just in a cool outer casing.

- He loves the human aspect! Vamp girls never blush or cuddle—there's nothing like the scent and softness of a warm-blooded girl.

- Real girls fascinate a vampire boy—they're so different from his own kind.

- Vamp lore is much more flexible and less cut-and-dried than I realized. He may be immortal, but he's definitely not mythical!

The Vampire Diaries III

Okay, so first-date nerves are long gone, but as you draw closer, you may be asking where this relationship will take you. Think through where the pair of you are, couple-wise (and where you'd like to be).

What his quiz told me about what he *really* thinks

....

....

....

....

....

Things he does I'm not so keen on

....

....

....

....

....

What I've learned about his hobbies...

....

....

....

....

....

...and the ones I'd take up too

....

....

....

....

....

How I feel

....

....

....

....

....

Long-Term Love

Weeks seem to have turned into months, and "going steady" has gradually become a full-on couple. People don't raise eyebrows at your passion for the pulseless anymore, but the novelty hasn't worn off for you either.

Dating a vampire still has its dilemmas. Can you take your vamp to the Prom? Does he do Thanksgiving? What do you buy the guy who's been around for centuries? And after all this time, how well do you really know each other?

Loving the Dark Side

Sick of hearing about blood, drama, and peril every time vamps hit the headlines? Sure, it's a thrill dating a vamp, but sometimes…it's kinda cozy, too.

Here are some everyday pluses your steady squeeze has over the warm-blooded.

He always…

- Understands the appeal of vintage movies.

- Notices if you've taken the time to make an effort.

- Goes along with you if you're in a quiet mood.

- Comes to the door to pick you up.

- Helps with your homework.

- Offers a cool, calm shoulder to cry on.

- Leaves you be if you need time alone.

- Keeps track of gossip you have mentioned.

- Has an opinion and stays cool about stating it.

- Arrives on time. This guy is killer punctual!

He never…

- Tries to make you watch sport on TV.

- Rolls his eyes if you're a bit late (he's got time…).

- Talks rubbish just for the sake of talking.

- Revs up to the door and honks the horn.

- Cancels your study dates.

- Tells you to calm down if you're upset.

- Accuses you of being moody when you want some space.

- Responds on autopilot—he chooses his words.

- Gets hot and bothered in an argument.

- Leaves you waiting, prey to other creatures of the night.

Quiz: How Well Do You Read Her? (Boys)

You're closer than crushes, sure, but are you made for each other? Are you too loved up to see the writing on the wall? Help your vamp-boy read your vital signs by getting him to answer these questions (your turn's over the page).

1 Do you think she gets a thrill out of your undead status?
a. Yes. I think it's the thing she likes best about me. ☆
b. Sometimes, although these days she often completely ☆
forgets about it.
c. Never. She loves me, but I know she wishes I was human. ☆

2 Does she feel limited by the things you can't do?
a. No way! When your boyfriend can fly, what's not to love? ☆
b. I think she sometimes longs for a warm-blooded hug. ☆
c. I know she'd love a day at the beach with me… ☆

3 Does she love your supernatural powers?
a. Yes. She's always asking to fly with me. ☆
b. She's curious, but doesn't want to hear *too* much ☆
about them.
c. No. They're strictly off-limits. ☆

4 Do you think she discusses you with her friends?

a. Yes. She's a major show-off about my powers.

b. Yes. I think she asks their opinion about dating me.

c. No. She's never told them that she dates me.

5 Does she think about your future together?

a. She seems to assume that we'll be together forever.

b. She's never mentioned it, but I think she worries about the age gap.

c. Yes. She frets about our afterlife together.

The signs spell...

Mostly As

This girl is your natural mate. She loves your nature and everything about it, and she's not afraid to show her feelings either.

Mostly Bs

She feels strongly for you, but she's in two minds about your immortal status. Long term, this could cause problems.

Mostly Cs

Have you noticed how she does her best to pretend that you're just like the other guys? Should the two of you talk?

Quiz: How Well Do You Read Him? (Girls)

Here we have your cheat sheet to working out what your boy's behavior tells you about your future as a toothsome twosome. Answer these questions to find out how mega-matched you really are.

1 How thirsty do you think you still make him?
a. Extremely. He can hardly keep his urge to bite in check.
b. Very, but he's under control.
c. Not at all. He's almost forgotten I'm not a vamp myself!

2 Does he get impatient when you can't keep up with his superspeed?
a. Absolutely! He'll wait for me, but it makes him bad tempered.
b. I think he sometimes wishes I could keep up with him.
c. Never. He relishes my human qualities.

3 What's most important to him?
a. That I'm good at keeping secrets.
b. That I can act as "cover" when he's out and about in the human world.
c. That I feel as strongly about him as he does about me.

4 How much do you see of his darker undead side?

a. He's open about it, but he'll pursue most full-on vamp activities on his own. ☆

b. I don't see too much up close, but he does take me flying. ☆

c. A lot. The only thing he won't do is take me hunting. ☆

5 Does he think about your future together?

a. He never talks about it. ☆

b. He'll talk about vacations or summer jobs—no further. ☆

c. Yes. He talks about being together forever. ☆

The signs spell...

Mostly As
Your boy's fully absorbed in his vamp identity. Are you really right for him, or should he be dating someone of his own blood group?

Mostly Bs
He definitely lives in the present. Is this because the pair of you have varying amounts of future to look forward to?

Mostly Cs
True love; but is he denying his true nature? Talk to your boy, before it gets out of hand.

High Days and Holidays

Do vamps do Christmas? Will you get a good Halloween surprise? Here's your cut-out 'n' keep guide to enjoying the holidays, vamp-style.

Prom

Past dates had to be forced into their tuxes and told to buy flowers, so you thought your ultra-cool vampire would have a bigger boy-aversion to formal dances and hired limos? Wrong.

Maybe he gets a blast from his past with the sense of tradition; maybe it's the chance to look dapper; maybe he just wants to dance with you all night, but whatever the reasons, vampires tend to love Prom. Not just the evening, but the buildup and dress-up, too. You'll have the biggest corsage and the best-looking boy, so relax and enjoy; it's your night to sparkle.

Halloween

All Hallows Eve. For once, he's not faking joining in with a human holiday—you're very definitely visiting one of his. Traditionally this is the night when the boundary between the worlds of the living and the dead disappears, so it's been authentic vamp territory for centuries (although the pumpkins and dress-up have taken over recently, so don't suggest bobbing for apples to your boy).

Forget trick and treating or witches' hats—ask your fella to take you for a walk on the wild side and see what he shows you. It's bound to be a lot more exciting than another trip around the neighborhood admiring the jack o'lanterns.

Vamp o'Lantern

Fanged Festivities

Christmas

This is probably the most difficult date for vampires to share in fully. There's the festive food and drink, the communal warmth and party atmosphere and the strictly family surroundings—and he's not a natural at any of them.

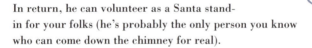

Eggnog won't appeal to his iron-starved palate, Twister's more foreign than Transylvania and most vamps don't have families of their own (or at least not in the conventional sense). Why not set aside Christmas Eve for private time?

In return, he can volunteer as a Santa stand-in for your folks (he's probably the only person you know who can come down the chimney for real).

Thanksgiving

The hardest thing about Thanksgiving is that it usually centers around a festive meal, but vamps aren't big eaters (at least not of turkey). How to deal with it? Skip the meal and ask him to come along afterwards. Then invent a date with his folks (whether or not he's part of a real vamp "family") so that he doesn't need to be on show for too long.

Even if your mom feels he needs feeding up ("He's lovely, but he's always *sooo* pale!"), make a stand. Just reassure her that you know he eats regularly, that you're certain he gets plenty of protein and that he's much, much stronger than he looks!

Valentine's Day

An event at which your vamp is 100% certain to shine. As with Prom, he has a wonderful sense of occasion and centuries of experience picking gifts and making romantic gestures (see pages 98–9 for what you might expect in the prezzie department).

If, up till now, your crushes were clueless about gifts, you've maybe racked back your expectations for fear of disappointment. Shelve your worries: you're dating the guy who is ready, willing and seriously able to take Valentine's a lot further than a mass-produced card and a limp bunch of petrol-station flowers! Prepare your own tribute, too—vamps are keen on getting, as well as giving.

Vampire Gifts I

Vamps aren't big on birthdays, but plenty of other occasions crop up through the year. So what do you choose for the boy who has everything...except a pulse?

What you might give him...

Get him

★ An exotic pet. Snakes and tarantulas are an obvious choice, as are bats and rats. Some of the fancier pet stores sell moth tanks with infrared goggles to watch their night wanderings with, and these might catch his fancy. You'll only need the specs if you want to watch too, though.

★ History books. A regular guy might groan if you bought him a dusty old tome for Christmas. Not so your vamp squeeze: they love history, particularly if they can remember it first hand. Go for true stories of witchcraft, the supernatural, and other dark deeds. He'll enjoy them the most, and you'll ace history class.

★ Plants for his garden. No, not daisies or dahlias! As with pets, go for the dark side of the herbal: deadly nightshade, poison ivy— that sort of thing. He'll find their unwholesome pallor and drooping foliage appealing.

Pass on

★ A classic red-lined cape. Vamps hate to be typecast, and even if he wore one back in the 17th century, he's had hundreds of years to get over that fashion *faux pas*.

★ Anything scented. Products might seem like the answer for a sophisticated modern boy, but most human scents (apart from the scent of humans themselves, that is) smell detestable to vamps. Steer clear.

★ Tickets for the match. Any match. Including the one your average boy would kill to get into. Vamps find human sports lame, even when played at uber-professional level, because by his standards, those players are moving at snail speed. Give them to your brother instead.

Vampire Gifts II

...And what he might give you

Jewelry

So far, so traditional. But his gifts won't be Christmas-cracker fare. Look forward to precious gems in polished settings—unless you're into boho styles, in which case you're more likely to be unwrapping a one-off from a bespoke boutique.

He'll consult your taste, for sure, but he'll be operating outside your budget. You'll know they're real, but you'll have to pretend they're fake to your family and friends.

Long-haul flights

...with or without aircraft! When your parents gave you permission to spend the summer hols together, they didn't envisage a trip by Vamp Air.

This guy's a planner, so he'll have worked out every last detail before you start, too. Just be prepared to travel very, very fast.

Heirloom trinkets

He may surprise you with something from his past. And what it is will depend on when he comes from. A gold-mounted snuffbox, a small silver bird- (or bat-) cage, a pearl-encrusted miniature...little things that you'll be able to treasure forever.

WHAT YOU WON'T BE UNWRAPPING

....

★ Anything involving crosses on chains.

★ Perfume. Why disguise your own irresistible scent?

★ A bouquet. Flowers are so overdone.

★ A puppy. You never know when he might want a snack.

Guy Talk

Did you ever wonder if he has a guide about how to date you? Here's just a handful of worries he shares with the rest of the vamp-boys about how to date a human!

How to behave around your folks

Vampires are aware that their manners seem too good to be true (thanks to their old-school strict upbringings). What do they confer on? How to hit the right balance between perfectly polite and just-a-bit-weird. No one, not even a vampire, wants to be regarded (even by your mother!) as too squeaky-clean for you to date.

What to do when you cry

Hopefully you don't do it all that often—because human tears can send a vamp into a spin. It's a little-known fact that tears are second only to blood on the vamp temptation list.

An often-asked question in vampire circles is will you think he's strange if he tries a taste? Luckily there's usually a seasoned vamp to set him straight, otherwise an over-emotional evening could turn plain creepy.

How to blend in

It's okay when he's with you—you share his secret. But in a group of warm-blooded people, he has to take care not to stand out. He and his mates constantly swap tips on how to merge most effectively: sunnies cover up giveaway dark-eye, while a program of carefully mapped movements makes sure his undead stillness is covered up.

Why girls are scary

It's ironic, really: while your friends are all worried and concerned about you vampire-dating, vamp-boys get together to talk about why girls make them nervous. Just like human boys, in fact!

The biggest vampire slayers? You're confident, you're usually surrounded by friends and you don't always fall at their feet for their century-old chat-up lines. See—you're not so different!

Time Apart

Even vamps take holidays! Whether you're seeing the world or kicking back and relaxing, if you're going your separate ways for a while, what's best to do?

For him

❧ An activity holiday, vamp-style. Team up with some vamp friends and really stretch those superskills.

❧ Charge up your levels of hemoglobin. Head off to the savanna and make the most of the all-you-can-eat buffet—while it's still on the hoof. Mmm…wildebeest.

❧ Take a cultural tour. Check out your ancestral homeland with a trip to Transylvania.

❧ Seek out one of the world's great woodworkers for a hand-crafted coffin. You may not choose to nap in it, but it's a great conversation piece for your pad!

For her

❧ Take a spa weekend. Smother yourself in as many perfumed lotions and scented scrubs as they'll give you: all those smells your boy hates.

❧ Head off on a horse trek. Vamps panic ponies, so while he's away you can enjoy a soothing one-to-one equine vibe.

❧ Get your fortune told. For once, he won't be there to spoil it by telling you what Mystic Meg is going to say before she says it!

❧ Take a gourmet trip. Sure, your guy's horror at human food has worked wonders on your waistline, but here's your chance to enjoy some meals out again.

THE VERDICT?
You're home, fresh and rested. Did absence make the heart grow fonder?

The Vampire Diaries IV

You've managed Prom, Valentine's, and even a family Thanksgiving without disaster, which is more than you've achieved with many a warm-blooded boy. So how do you feel?

How's he coping without the first-date flutters?

....

....

....

....

....

Does it look like his feelings are growing?

....

....

....

....

....

Does he ever frighten me?

....

....

....

....

....

How much have I learned about his history?

....

....

....

....

....

How I feel

....

....

....

....

Happy Ever After?

So, could this love last forever? "Till death us do part" means nothing to a vampire, because it ain't going to happen. Will he watch you get a little older every year? Can you face turning vamp? Someday soon, you'll hit the stage where something's gotta give.

But it's not all doom and gloom! You've come this far, and whatever happens in this rollercoaster relationship, would you have passed on all that romance and all those adventures? We doubt it!

Getting Serious: Your Vampire's Clan

Your first introduction to your vamp's closest clan (technically called a "kiss"—cute, but kinda creepy) is a big deal. Your boy's paved the way raving about you, but they don't want to see him get hurt, so first impressions definitely count.

Do

★ Take a gift. Don't bother with flowers or chocs, though. Go to your nearest crystal store and splash out on a lump of amethyst or aquamarine. Vamps love them. (They like ruby, too, but it's a bit much for a first visit.)

★ Eat before you go. There (hopefully) won't be a meal on the table and the company will tactfully avoid any mention of hunger or thirst.

★ Dress for the occasion. Ask your guy what the plans for the evening are.

★ And remember, your passport to your fella's friends is the fact he thinks a lot of you. So if he likes you, the chances are they'll think you're just as appealing as he does—as a person, rather than a snack food.

Don't

★ Chatter. Older vamps are quite serious types; you don't want them to put you down as an airhead.

★ Fidget. Vamps are naturally still, so you'll be drawing attention to yourself and your human qualities. Not too wise.

★ Gush. Vampires often live in surroundings of considerable splendor (remember all those investments they've had decades to build up). Behave as though you fit right in, even if your jaw wants to hit the floor. Relax, and they're bound to love you!

Exit Lines

As any vamp-lovin' girl will know, once or twice you get that sudden sense that your guy has changed—from partner to predator. When you have to leave, here's how to make a super-speedy escape.

Spotting the signs

Darker eyes

Vamp eyes glisten and are a beautiful pale color when relaxed. When he's thirsty, however, his pupils widen and his eyes darken, through a Drac-classic red to deepest black, if he's parched. Keep your eyes on his, and take off before they've gone dark for danger.

A stronger smell

Vamps smell gorgeous to the human nose; the scent is a part of their super-seductive qualities. If you notice his fragrance is suddenly stronger, it's a sign that your vamp is getting worked up, so get gone!

Acting distracted

It's the rhythmic beating of a pulse that can catch—and keep—his gaze. If you find he's staring at your neck or your wrist, you need to distract him fast, or be ready to make a rapid getaway. He's not admiring your jewelry.

Averting a crisis

Call in the cavalry

Enlist a (human) friend. Text or tweet for reinforcements. Vamps isolate their prey; there's safety in numbers.

Flower power

Buy some time by baffling his senses. Keep a perfume atomizer filled with something strong (this isn't the moment for a delicate floral) in your bag. Spray yourself lavishly and leg it while he's still spluttering.

Stink him out

If he seems in a funny or distracted mood, pre-prep. Have a handkerchief full of garlic cloves to hand in your pocket. If he starts to stare and isn't listening, take it out and rub garlic lavishly on your pulse points. As he tries to work out where the smell's coming from, head for the restroom and leave by the back entrance.

Cooling off

Make sure the mood's changed before you see him again. Act responsibly for the pair of you—because he can't help what he is, and he can't always control it.

Quiz: Keeper or Quitter?

He's (eternally) young, bright, and gorgeous, but is he yours forever? You don't want to rock the boat, but it's natural to wonder whether you'll still be together in a few months' time. Take our quiz to find out if your vamp's a lifetime lover or a goodtime guy.

1 You're out together and you run into a bunch of his undead pals. What does he do?

a. Holds you even closer, says hi, then passes quickly by. ☆

b. Stops for a quick chat about vamp stuff. ☆

c. High-fives his mates, then launches into hunting plans. ☆

d. Pretends he isn't with you. ☆

2 There's a big test tomorrow, so you need to hit the books. How does your vamp help?

a. He comes round to coach you through it. ☆

b. He'll test you for an hour, then leave you in peace. ☆

c. He tells you that that's fine—he wanted a night off. ☆

d. He suggests you should stay at home and study more often. ☆

3 How does he field a family dinner date?

a. He'll happily come and fake the feeding. ☆

b. He joins you after the meal to spend the evening with your family without hurting anyone's feelings. ☆

c. He pops round to say hi to the folks, then makes his excuses. ☆

d. Sends your mom his apologies, through you. ☆

4 He's suggested an overnight flight, but you're feeling a little fragile. What does he do?

a. Suggests you stop where you are and camp for the night. ☆

b. Coaxes you just a little further to get to the best campsite. ☆

c. Acts impatient until you agree to fly on. ☆

d. Takes you home in a sulk, then doesn't call for days. ☆

5 Your much-loved pet pup is frightened of your fella. How does he deal with it?

a. Pets her until she forgets he doesn't smell quite right. ☆

b. Steers clear—he doesn't like to frighten her. ☆

c. Suggests you shut her away when he's visiting. ☆

d. Makes jokes (you hope) about her being a snack. ☆

6 It's your guy's "becoming" day (the day he turned vamp) and you bought him a ring to celebrate. What does he do?

a. Hugs you, puts it on and says he'll never take it off. ☆

b. Thanks you warmly and tries it on. ☆

c. Unwraps it, then puts it in his pocket "to keep safe." ☆

d. Takes it out, says thanks, then changes the subject. ☆

Answers: Keeper or Quitter?

Mostly As

This vamp's a keeper. You've warmed his chilly heart and he cares deeply about you and everything to do with you. His commitment isn't in question and he'd fry in the sun before he'd let anything harm you. If you feel just as strongly, it's time to discuss your future together, because it's hard to think of a force powerful enough to tear you two apart.

Mostly Bs

In vampire terms, this fella is a steady Eddie. He's sensible, grounded, and affectionate, and he looks after his own needs as well as yours. Far from typical, he's a safe bet in the long term—but if the reason you fancied a vamp in the first place was that you craved drama, romance and a distinctly dangerous edge to life, you'll be disappointed. This character's definitely at the dependable end of the undead scale!

Mostly Cs

A little bit flighty, a little bit scary—this guy has all the vampire attractions, but they're mixed with a strong pinch of selfishness. He likes you—he may even love you—but everything with this vamp is on his own terms. If you have strong feelings for him, be very careful: his self-centered approach could mean you make a lot of compromises and still end up getting burned. More quitter than keeper, so tread cautiously.

Mostly Ds

You already knew the answer, right? You're kidding yourself if you think he spares you a moment's thought when you're not with him. However long you've been dating, this boy thinks only of himself. His supernatural cool goes way below skin deep: he doesn't care about you or anything you feel strongly about. Chuck him now, before he quits.

Calling it Quits

However crazy you were about him, something's lost its sparkle. If you can't bring the magic back, how are you going to say good-bye?

Break it gently

One thing's for sure, it won't come as a surprise. The moment you knew you were breaking up with him, so did he. Those mind-reading skills sure can be pesky. He may be able to hear your thoughts, but run through the script anyway, and cushion your news by telling him how special he's been to you. Ask if you should call one of his cold-blooded friends to come over. Vamps understand vamps, and he'll want one of his own kind to confide in.

Pick your moment

Choose your location. The school corridor isn't private enough; your favorite spot deep in the woods is *too* private. At home, the park, or a quiet café (not his fave—don't ruin it for him!) are better choices.

Face to face

Be brave and do it in person. Texts, e-mails, and Facebook weren't invented for the uber-emotional moments in life. Even though he can read your feelings before you voice them, you still need to say them out loud to show you're serious.

Saying sayonara

When it comes to the crunch, vamps aren't different from human boys. Straight off, he may not be able to agree to be friends, and face it, do you really want quality time with a distraught vamp anyway? He may start looking at you differently, and not in a good way!

I suggest you don't see each other for a week or two. Remember, he's got all the time in the world to sort himself out, so it's best to focus on what is right for you…and seeing him won't help.

The End of the Affair

It's happened to us all. Without any warning (you're not a mind reader, after all), he draws you aside and tells you he doesn't think it's working out.

How do you handle being dumped?

Golden rules

Take the news calmly, whatever happens. Don't cry—vamps love tears and you don't want to make him thirsty. Plus, shouting "So long, sucker!" and storming out won't feel so great an hour later.

Don't stick around to say too much—he already knows how you feel, and you definitely don't want to beg! The quicker you can take the news in, the sooner you'll find that you're feeling surprisingly positive about being single again!

What next?

After any breakup you need a little downtime. Spend a day or two moping and eating chocolate, then call some girlfriends for an in-house spa session. After a full mani-pedi and an hour or two's gossip about who's freshly on the dating scene, you'll feel not just ready but positively eager to face the world again.

Moving forward

Even if you're looking forward to the dating smorgasbord that awaits you, take a week or two out to enjoy your independence before jumping

back into the dating world. Be cautious with the next guys who ask: if you were intrepid enough for a vamp, you may get a werewolf or a warlock trying their luck!

For a bit of fun and romance on a Saturday night, you could revisit the world of warm-blooded boys for a bit. And if you find human boys just don't cut it after your fanged fella's high standards, you can always go out hunting vampires again. You've learned the rules for vamp-dating—you may as well put them to use!

MAKE THE MOST OF IT!

Dealing with a vamp will have made you super-savvy in the ways of nonhuman relationships. Why not give back to the community with an online "Dear Abby" column for those who, like you, enjoy dating outside the box.

Long-Term Love?

It's not all a question of what's written in the stars; a lot of dating is down to checks and balances. There are plenty of reasons to stay together, but only some of them are good...

Check which column sounds more like you before heading out on your happy-ever-after.

Forever after

Nice knowing you

It's for real

- You have strong feelings for him as a person.

- You can look after yourself, but can't imagine what life would be like without him.

- He's independent and knows what he wants.

- There's a strong mental connection between you.

- You're convinced you're meant to be together.

- Your friends are his friends, and vice versa.

- You love him.

- He's smart; you've learned a lot from him.

- You feel totally safe with him.

You're kidding yourself

- Having vamp-girlfriend status is super-cool.

- He's the best bodyguard you could have! And handsome with it!

- He's rich—and really good at presents.

- His psychic powers give him control over you.

- He's convinced you're meant to be together.

- You come as a pair; you don't need anyone else.

- Your mom loves him.

- He's super-smart; he helps you cruise through class.

- He's dangerous!

THE VERDICT?

Will you stick or quit? If it's true love, congrats! But if not, just think "Fangs for the memory!"—it was still the romance of a lifetime.

The Vampire Diaries V

Whether you've chosen to stick with your guy or say your good-byes, you may be wondering whether anything you did or said could have made a difference. Made a mistake, or a lucky escape? You decide…

How's my social life doing?

....

....

....

....

....

What have I learned about vamps *and* boys?

....

....

....

....

....

What about the future?

....

....

....

....

Would I ever date another vamp?

....

....

....

....

....

How I feel

....

....

....

....

Index

Index

Publisher Ljiljana Baird
Managing Editor Camilla Davis
Project Editor Kate Fox
Designer Michelle Tilly
Illustrator Michelle Tilly
Production Manager
    Caroline Alberti